Wizards Don't Need Computers

by Debbie Dadey
and
Marcia Thornton Jones

illustrated by John Steven Gurney

A
LITTLE **APPLE**
PAPERBACK

SCHOLASTIC INC.
New York Toronto London Auckland Sydney

ISBN 0-590-50962-4

22   4 5 6 7 8 9/0

Printed in the U.S.A.   40

First Scholastic printing, March 1996

Book design by Laurie Williams

For Walter Jones and Charles Dadey

Contents

Wizards Don't Need Computers

1

Fit for a King

"I can't believe we have to do this," Eddie complained.

"I think doing a report about England will be fun," Liza said. "It's a fascinating place with lots of history." Eddie and Liza were on the steps of the public library with their friends Howie and Melody.

"I'm only in third grade," Eddie complained again, pulling off his baseball cap. "I shouldn't have to go to the public library more than once a year. It's bad for my health. I should be out in the fresh air playing."

Melody pushed her black pigtails out of her face and stared up at the huge library building. Six large gargoyle statues looked down from the roof. "I don't

1

mind going to the library since they fixed it up," she said.

Howie nodded. "It is neat. They even have tons of new books and computers."

"If they really wanted to make it neat," Eddie told them as he pulled open the heavy library door, "they'd add an indoor soccer area and pinball machines."

Liza giggled. "Whoever heard of a library with pinball machines?"

Eddie stopped at the door and stared inside the library. "Whoever heard of a library with an ocean inside?"

"What?" Liza, Melody, and Howie asked together.

Eddie didn't say a word, he just pointed. The four friends looked at where he pointed and gasped.

"Where did that come from?" Melody whispered.

Eddie grinned. "Who cares? This is better than a soccer field!"

Eddie rushed across the lobby to the

librarians' counter to get a closer look. His three friends followed. A glass aquarium took up the entire wall behind the counter. Tiny gray, silver, and blue fish darted around, but one huge goldfish slowly circled a colorful ceramic castle resting on the bottom of the aquarium.

"I've never seen an aquarium that big," Eddie said. "It's fit for a king!"

"Of course it is," a deep voice with a strange accent said. "Arthur deserves a kingdom."

Eddie, Melody, Howie, and Liza whirled around to face the stranger. His white hair reached his collar and he had a long pointed beard. He wore a dark blue turtleneck shirt and around his neck dangled a silver star necklace. The stranger smiled at the four kids.

"Who is Arthur, and who are you?" Eddie asked.

"I'm the new library assistant, Mr.

Merle," he said. "And Arthur is that ma-jestic goldfish." Mr. Merle pointed to the lone goldfish floating near the castle.

"That's the biggest tank I've ever seen," Liza said.

"And Arthur is the biggest goldfish I've ever seen," Howie said.

Melody nodded. "It must have taken you a week just to set up that aquarium."

"For me, it was a snap," Mr. Merle said, snapping his fingers. Then he walked behind the librarian's counter to sprinkle some fish food into the aquarium. He had to climb up on a stool to reach the top.

Howie tugged at Liza's and Melody's elbows to get their attention. He put a finger to his lips for quiet and led them across the library into the science fiction section. Eddie trotted after his friends.

"What's wrong with you?" Melody asked.

"That fish tank wasn't there the last time I checked out a book," Howie told them. "And that was just yesterday."

Eddie's eyes were round. "You came to the library yesterday? Why?"

"To check out a book," Howie repeated.

Eddie rolled his eyes. "No wonder you're upset. You're spending way too much time in this library."

"That's not the problem," Howie snapped. "An aquarium that size takes a long time to put up. Mr. Merle's aquarium wasn't there yesterday."

"You heard Mr. Merle," Liza said. "For him it's a snap."

"Or," Howie said slowly, "there's something fishy in Bailey City!"

2

Camelot

"We'd better find books for our reports," Liza reminded her friends.

Howie nodded. "I'll check the card catalogue for England."

Mr. Merle popped his head over a huge pile of books. "Sorry, kids, the card catalogue is closed. We're putting everything into computers."

"Then how can we find a book?" Melody asked.

"We're doing reports on something about England," Howie explained. "I want to learn about King Arthur."

Mr. Merle smiled and stroked his long white beard. "Ah, yes, Camelot," he said.

"Camelot?" Liza asked.

"Yes," Mr. Merle told them, "Camelot was King Arthur's kingdom."

"That stuff about King Arthur and the Knights of the Round Table is all made up," Eddie said.

Mr. Merle's face got bright red. "Nothing could be further from the truth. Camelot was a magical place, but it was as real as I am."

Howie tapped Mr. Merle on the shoulder. "How can I find a book about King Arthur without the card catalogue?"

"No problem," Mr. Merle said. "There's a wonderful book called *Arthur and Camelot*. I'll check the computer to see if it's here."

Mr. Merle sat down and typed something into the computer, but the head librarian, Mrs. Farley, shook her finger at the kids. "Sorry, boys and girls, but that book was lost two years ago."

Mr. Merle waved his hands over the

keys, touched his beard, then snapped his fingers and smiled. "*Arthur and Camelot* shows up on the computer. I'll go check the shelves."

The four kids followed Mr. Merle to the shelves of books. Eddie stopped in the sports section to look while Mr. Merle and the other kids went directly to the literature section.

"Here it is," Mr. Merle said, pulling a large blue book off the shelf. "This has always been one of my favorites."

"This is more my style," Eddie said from behind them. He grinned and held up a tall thin book with big red letters spelling *Soccer*.

"Eddie," Liza said, "you're supposed to find a book about England, not soccer."

"Actually," Mr. Merle told the kids, "in England, the game you call soccer is called football. Football is a very popular sport in England. I think it would be an excellent topic for your report."

"All right!" Eddie said, "England must be a magical place after all."

Mr. Merle nodded his head, rubbed his beard, and smiled. "Indeed, it is very magical, as I'm sure you will find out very soon."

3

King Arthur's Wizard

"This book about King Arthur is fantastic!" Howie told his friends the next afternoon after school. They were in their favorite meeting place under the big oak tree on the playground.

"Who cares?" Eddie said. "If I have to read a book, it should be one about something interesting. Like sports."

Howie ignored Eddie and kept talking. "King Arthur and his wizard, Merlin, created the kingdom of Camelot. They had all these loyal Knights of the Round Table who were dedicated to doing good. Check out these drawings."

Melody and Liza gathered close to the book. "Oh, look at that castle," Liza said. "It's so romantic. I wish I had chosen

Camelot instead of London for my report."

"King Arthur sure seems more interesting than the Tower of London," Melody said.

"Who is this beautiful lady?" Liza asked Howie.

"That's a drawing of Guinevere, the Queen of Camelot," Howie explained. "She was the most beautiful lady in all the land."

"That Mr. Merle is a little different," Melody said, turning the pages of Howie's book, "but he was right about Camelot being magical."

"He may be weird," Howie agreed, "but he sure knows his stuff. He found my book using the library computer in just two seconds."

Liza gasped and pointed to a drawing.

"What's wrong with you?" Eddie asked. "Book got your tongue?"

Liza didn't say anything. She just kept pointing to Howie's book. Melody, Howie, and Eddie gathered closer to see.

"Oh, my gosh," Melody whispered. "Look at that drawing!"

4

Merlin the Wizard

"That drawing of King Arthur's wizard looks just like Mr. Merle!" Melody said.

Howie put his nose close to the picture to get a better look. The wizard had wavy white hair and a long pointed beard. A star necklace hung around the famous wizard's neck and he wore a navy blue robe. A pointy hat was perched on the wizard's head. "You're right," Howie said, "Mr. Merle looks like Merlin the Wizard. Mr. Merle even has a necklace like Merlin!"

Liza let out a scream and Melody dropped the book. Howie jumped back and Eddie put up his fists, ready to fight.

"Why did you scream?" Melody gasped.

"I'm sorry," Liza told her friends. "But

"MERLIN"

I just realized Mr. Merle's name sounds like Merlin."

Melody's eyes were big. "And his fish's name is Arthur, as in King Arthur!"

"Maybe," Howie said slowly, "maybe . . . Mr. Merle is Merlin."

Liza and Melody gulped, but Eddie just laughed. "Bailey City's new library assistant is no wizard," he said. "Wizards use magic to get whatever they want. They don't have to work shelving books in libraries. And they definitely don't need computers!"

"Eddie's right," Melody said. "King Arthur wasn't a fish. Besides, why would King Arthur and the great wizard Merlin come to Bailey City? It's nothing like Camelot."

Howie nodded. "You're right about that. Camelot was a beautiful and peaceful kingdom."

"So is Bailey City," Liza said softly.

Liza's three friends stared at her for a

full minute before Howie finally spoke. "You must be King Arthur's foolish court jester if you think Bailey City is a beautiful and peaceful place."

Eddie pointed his finger at Liza. "Bailey City is an old-fashioned dump. There are no skyscrapers or speeding subways."

"Those things don't matter," Melody argued. "Trees and flowers make a city pretty—"

"Friendly people make a city beautiful,"

Liza interrupted. "And Bailey City is full of nice people."

Eddie laughed. "Bailey City is full of people, but they're all strange," he told her. "Just like Mr. Merle."

"He's not strange," Howie pointed out, "for a wizard!"

"But he's not a wizard. I don't believe in wizards," Eddie said. "I don't even believe in magic."

"I believe in magic," Liza said softly. But her friends were too busy arguing to hear.

5

Wizard's Spells

Eddie had his hands on his hips. "It would be easy to prove Mr. Merle is no magician!"

"How?" Melody demanded to know.

"We'll go to the library and do a little research of our own," Eddie told them matter-of-factly.

"I think I'm going to faint," Liza said. "Since when does Eddie want to do research?"

"He means he wants to do a little snooping," Melody said.

"Researching, snooping," Eddie said. "Either way, I'll find out Mr. Merle is just a harmless bookworm who likes fish."

"We could be in great danger if Eddie's wrong," Howie warned. "A powerful wiz-

ard like Merlin could stir up a dangerous potion."

"The only thing Mr. Merle can stir up is a fish tank." Eddie laughed. "And I'll prove it."

Eddie stomped toward the Bailey City Library. His three friends had to hurry to keep up. Liza shivered when they reached the shadows of the giant gargoyles perched on the library's roof.

"This isn't such a great idea," Melody whispered. "We'll get in trouble if we're caught."

"We'll be worse than in trouble," Howie warned. "We'll be caught in a wizard's spell."

"I think you're already stuck in an idiot spell." Eddie laughed. "Now quit stalling and follow me."

Eddie tiptoed into the library and past the librarians' counter. He paused long enough to see a lone sunbeam glint off the scales of the goldfish. Then Eddie, with his three friends following close on his heels, sneaked behind the counter and into the deserted librarians' office. None of them noticed that the giant goldfish had stopped circling the castle to stare straight at the four sneaky kids.

Eddie found Mr. Merle's desk. It was piled high with big dusty books. "A wizard's desk would be full of magic things," Eddie told his friends. "Obviously, Mr. Merle's desk is not."

Then Eddie pulled open a desk drawer. "Don't do that," Liza hissed. "It's private property."

Howie gulped. "No, I'd say it's *magic* property."

"What are you talking about?" Melody said. Then she stared inside the drawer. None of the four kids said a word.

"Is that what I think it is?" Liza whispered, pointing to a gleaming glass ball that was nestled beside a long, shiny blue wand.

"If that's not a crystal ball, then I'm a monkey's uncle," Howie said.

Eddie laughed and reached for the ball. "No wonder you like bananas so much."

"Don't touch that!" Melody screeched. "What if it *is* magic?"

"Wait! Someone is coming," Howie said. "What if it's Mr. Merle?"

The four kids ducked under the large desk and waited.

6

Swirlin' Merlin

Holding their breaths, all four kids crawled around Mr. Merle's desk and out of the librarians' office. They scooted around one side of the checkout counter while Mr. Merle came in on the other side. The four kids huddled together on the floor with their backs to the fish tank.

"Whew!" Liza whispered. "That was close."

Howie put his finger to his lips and pointed to the fish tank. Arthur the goldfish was staring at them. "We're not safe yet," Howie said. "Follow me."

The kids crawled past the checkout counter and the sports section to the literature section. In front of the King Arthur books they sprawled on the floor.

"I thought Mr. Merle was going to smash us to smithereens," Melody said softly.

"Wizards don't smash anyone," Liza told her. "Wizards probably whisk you away to a faraway place like Alaska."

Eddie shook his head. "Just because we found that ball and stick, it doesn't mean that Mr. Merle is Swirlin' Merlin the Weird Wizard."

"That's true," Melody said, "maybe that stuff is for a costume party."

"It looked real to me," Liza said.

"We never did figure out why a wizard would come here to Bailey City anyway," Melody said, leaning against the book-shelf.

"To bring back Camelot," Howie said.

29

"That would be great." Liza giggled and pulled out a book with a big castle on the front.

"Only if you think knights fighting duels on the soccer field is great," Howie argued.

"I guess you're right," Liza said, looking at the castle picture. "I've heard those castles were cold and drafty."

"That's because they didn't have any heat except for fireplaces," Melody explained. Then she looked at Eddie. "They didn't have electricity either, so they didn't have computer games."

"I don't care about knights or castles," Eddie told them. "And most of all I don't care about wizards."

"You'll care if Mr. Merle transforms Bailey City into a medieval kingdom," Howie said.

"He won't," Eddie said. "Because he isn't a wizard."

"How can you be so sure?" Melody asked.

"Because there aren't any wizards," Eddie said, "and there never have been!"

"I wouldn't be so sure of that," said a voice from behind Eddie.

7

Queen of England

Liza grabbed Melody's arm and Howie gulped loudly. All four kids peered up at a very old lady with long silver hair pulled back by a glittering headband. "I happen to believe in wizards," she said.

"Who are you?" Eddie blurted.

When the strange woman smiled, her blue eyes sparkled. "I'm Mrs. Queen. I came to help in the library as soon as I

heard Mr. Merle was in town. He is an old, dear friend."

Mrs. Queen sighed and got a faraway look in her eyes. "It's been such a long, long time since I've seen my friends. We had so much fun back then!" She smiled brightly at the four friends huddled on the floor.

"Who are you talking about?" Melody asked.

"Why, Mr. Merle and Arthur," Mrs. Queen said matter-of-factly before disappearing behind a shelf filled with encyclopedias.

"Isn't it nice when people stay friends for a long time?" Liza asked Eddie, Howie, and Melody. "I hope we're still friends when we're that old."

"Not if I can help it," Eddie kidded.

"I wonder how long Mr. Merle and Mrs. Queen have been friends," Melody said.

"Not that long," Howie said slowly, "only about fifteen hundred years!"

"What?" his three friends asked.

"Don't you get it?" Howie asked. "That was Mrs. *Queen*. As in the *Queen* of England!"

"What would the Queen of England be doing shelving books in Bailey City?" Melody asked.

"You heard her," Howie said. "She came to be with Mr. Merle and Arthur, her husband!"

"There's something royal in Bailey City, all right." Eddie laughed. "But it's a royal pain. And that's you."

"Eddie's right," Liza said softly. "People don't live to be fifteen hundred years old."

"And queens don't marry goldfish!" Melody giggled.

"They can with a little help from a wizard," Howie said seriously.

Howie ignored his friends' laughter. Instead, he opened his library book. "It's all right here," he said, flipping through the pages to the back. "King Arthur never

died. He disappeared. And so did his trusted wizard, Merlin. They were last seen boarding a boat to the magical island of Avalon. Before King Arthur left, he promised to use Merlin's magic to return, and his wife, Guinevere, vowed to wait for him."

Howie looked each of his friends in the eyes. "I believe her long wait is over. Merlin has brought King Arthur back and they're all right here in the Bailey City Library."

"Well, I'm getting out of this library," Eddie said. "We've been here all day." He jumped up from the floor. "I plan to forget all this wizard stuff on the playground." Howie, Melody, and Liza scrambled to follow Eddie as he marched out of the literature section, past sports, and past the counter where Mrs. Queen was handing Mr. Merle a stack of books.

"Thank you so much," Mr. Merle was saying. And then he said something that made Eddie run out the door.

8

Dark Ages

"Why did you run all the way here?" Liza asked. The four kids were panting underneath the oak tree on the playground.

"Yeah," Melody gasped. "You'd think a ghost was chasing you."

"It was," Eddie said softly, kicking some dirt with his tennis shoe.

Howie dropped his backpack on the ground and looked at Eddie. "What are you talking about?"

Eddie leaned against the oak tree. "Didn't you hear what Mr. Merle called Mrs. Queen?"

Melody, Howie, and Liza shook their heads.

"He called her Guinevere," Eddie said.

Liza gulped. "Isn't that the name of King Arthur's wife?"

Howie snapped his fingers. "I knew it! Mrs. Queen really is from Camelot."

"Hold on there," Eddie said, holding up his hand. "Don't get carried away. I'm sure there are lots of people with that name."

"I've never known anyone with that name," Melody said.

"Me neither," Liza admitted. "Besides you must have thought she was Queen Guinevere or you wouldn't have run."

"I was just surprised," Eddie said. "That's all. Anyway, she can't be the same woman. The Guinevere in Howie's book was young and beautiful. Mrs. Queen looks older than dirt."

Howie picked up his backpack and slung it over his shoulder. "You'd be old too if you lived in King Arthur's days."

Eddie rolled his eyes. "Well, I'm not old — I'm young and I want to play. I'm tired of wizards and crazy queens. Let's play soccer."

"Not me," Howie said. "I'm going back to the library to find out the truth."

"The truth is that you're nuts," Eddie told him. "I'm not a library yo-yo. I've had it with bouncing back and forth to the library."

Melody and Liza walked away with Howie. Melody looked over her shoulder.

"You'd better come with us," she said, "or you'll be left in the dark."

"You mean the dark ages," Eddie muttered and sighed. But he followed his friends without another complaint.

When the kids got to the library they didn't go in. They just stood staring at the front steps. "Oh, my gosh," Liza whispered. "What happened?"

9

Kingdom

"Holy Toledo!" Eddie shouted. "It looks like the library fell into a time machine."

"And we've ended up in Camelot," Melody said. The four kids stared at the library steps with their mouths open. Red pointed banners draped the stair railings and ladies in long dresses with funny pointed hats waved to them. There was even a man walking about in a suit of armor.

Mr. Merle opened the library door and smiled at them. "Welcome to my kingdom," he said.

Howie gulped. "Your kingdom?"

"Certainly," Mr. Merle said, touching his star necklace. "Isn't it delightful? Just like Camelot."

"But we were just here," Liza said. "And none of this was on the steps."

"Nobody can work that fast," Melody said softly.

"Oh, it just took a wave of my fingers," Mr. Merle said with a chuckle. "I've always been very good with my hands."

Howie looked at Melody and winked. Mr. Merle taped a large sign beside the door. In big red letters it said: KINGDOM OF READING.

"What's that?" Liza asked.

"My new reading program to encourage kids to read," Mr. Merle told them.

"Nothing can encourage Eddie to read," Melody said.

Mr. Merle looked at Eddie and rubbed his long white beard. "Perhaps a little magic from my kingdom will do the trick."

"I don't believe in magic," Eddie told him.

Mr. Merle's face turned red. "What?

Magic is everywhere and especially in reading. Books can transport you to any time and any place."

"The only place I want to be is on the soccer field," Eddie complained.

Mr. Merle waved his fingers toward Eddie and smiled. "Magic is everywhere. Just wait and see."

10

Magic Mush

"Where's Eddie?" Melody asked.

"On the soccer field," Liza said. "Everybody that's not reading is there."

It had been a whole week since Mr. Merle started his new reading program. Melody, Howie, and Liza huddled under the giant oak tree that shaded their brand-new playground. But nobody was using the dragon-shaped sliding board or jumping over the rubber tire moat surrounding their play castle. Instead, kids had raced after school to find a comfortable spot to read.

"It looks like Mr. Merle's kingdom reaches all the way to Bailey Elementary," Melody said.

"Ever since Mr. Merle started his Kingdom of Reading nobody's been using

our brand-new playground," Howie said, pointing to a group of third-graders sitting on the swings. But they weren't swinging. They were too busy reading.

"It's almost eerie." Melody shivered. "It's a good thing Eddie's not here to see this. It would make him madder than a knight in rusted armor."

"I think it's a good idea. The person who reads the most wins a crown," Liza said. "As a matter-of-fact, I've been reading, too." When Liza held up her book about magic, Howie gasped.

"Where did you get that?" he asked.

Liza smiled. "Mr. Merle found it for me. He just waved his fingers and pulled it off a shelf. I sure was lucky, because it's a great book."

"Luck has nothing to do with it," Howie told her. "This reading craze is the work of magic. Merle Magic."

"But you like to read," Melody interrupted. "You should be glad everyone's reading. Even if it is magic, reading is good magic."

"I've got nothing against reading, but I do have a problem with a loony wizard taking over Bailey City," Howie said as he stomped away from his two friends.

"Where are you going?" Melody asked.

"To find Eddie," Howie called over his shoulder. "And to get away from this reading rage." Liza and Melody hurried after Howie.

They found Howie standing in the middle of the deserted soccer field. Some soccer players sat on the nearby bleachers. Every one of them was reading. Howie stomped up to the group. "Where's Eddie?" he asked.

"Shhh," several kids said, "we're reading."

"I can't believe it!" Howie said as he stomped around the bleachers with Melody and Liza following.

There they found Eddie curled up,

reading a fat book. Eddie grinned at his friends. "This is the greatest book," he told them. "It's the history of soccer. I'm going to read this one next," he said, pointing to another book. "It's about a famous soccer player from Brazil!"

"Two books?" Howie gasped. "You're reading two fat books?"

Eddie nodded. "And I need to hurry. Mr. Merle showed me a whole shelf filled with soccer books. It's funny how I never

saw them before. Mr. Merle just waved his fingers and there they were!" Eddie turned away from his friends and continued reading.

Howie pulled Liza and Melody away from the bleachers. "This is not normal for Eddie. Mr. Merle's magic has turned Eddie to mush! We have to do something. And fast!"

11

King Arthur's Paradise

Howie grabbed Liza's book. "Do you really believe in this magic stuff?"

Liza nodded. "I've always believed in magic tricks."

"Then it's time to make a little magic of our own," Howie told his friends.

"How do we do that?" Melody asked.

"Easy." Howie grinned. "Just follow me." Then he jogged off the soccer field and straight to the library. They stopped to catch their breaths when they reached the old building.

"Isn't that Mrs. Queen?" Liza asked. She pointed to a park bench across the street from the library. She held hands with a man dressed in a deep purple velvet jogging suit.

"I've never seen that man before," Melody said.

"Of course not," Howie told her. "Nobody's seen King Arthur for centuries."

"King Arthur?" Melody asked. "I thought Arthur was Mr. Merle's goldfish."

"He was," Howie said. "But it looks like Mr. Merle, the king's personal wizard, has brought him back to be with Guinevere. Just like King Arthur promised."

"You don't know that for sure," Melody whispered as they entered the silent library.

"Oh, yeah," Howie hissed back. "Then explain that!" He pointed to the giant fish tank behind the librarians' counter. Thirteen tiny silver, gray, and blue fish swam in circles. But the giant goldfish was gone.

"Maybe it died," Liza said. "That's what happened to my goldfish."

"Mr. Merle's goldfish wasn't just an ordinary fish," Howie said. "It was the famous King of England. And now he's come to take over Bailey City. Look around you for proof."

Liza and Melody turned in a circle to get a better look at the Bailey City Library. Bright streamers were draped from the ceiling and ladies in flowing dresses and pointy hats glided across the floor.

"Maybe it will be nice living in King Arthur's paradise," Liza said softly.

"That's what the Knights of the Round Table thought," Howie said. "But they found out there is no such thing as paradise. Their battles brought an end to King Arthur's kingdom, and they'll bring an end to Bailey City if we let Mr. Merle's magic bring them back to life. Now, let's go."

Howie stomped right into the librarians' office. He pulled open Mr. Merle's desk drawer and grabbed the shiny blue wand.

"What are you doing?" Liza gasped.

"I'm borrowing a little of Mr. Merle's magic," Howie said. Then he marched out of the office.

Mr. Merle stood at the top of the stairs leading to the biography section. As soon as he saw Howie with the wand, he pointed a gnarled finger at Howie and yelled, "*Stop!*"

But he was too late. Howie waved the wand in large circles.

12

Brief Shining Moment

"I thought you were toast," Melody told Howie the next day. Eddie, Liza, Melody, and Howie sat on the bench across from the library. Eddie was reading his second soccer book.

Liza nodded. "We were lucky," Liza said. "Mr. Merle just yelled because the wand is old and priceless. He could have zapped us."

"I know," Howie said.

"All Mr. Merle had to do was wave his magic fingers and that would have been the end of you," Melody said.

"You could have been turned into boiled eye of newt!" Liza added.

Melody laughed and pulled her knees

close to her body. "Here's Howie as a boiled eyeball."

Liza giggled and looked at Eddie. He was still reading. Usually he would have jumped at the chance to tease Howie, but Eddie didn't take his eyes off his book.

"We may end up worse than that." Howie sighed. "They're talking about postponing the beginning of soccer camp until Mr. Merle's Kingdom of Reading is finished."

"No!" Melody said, jumping up from her seat. "That's no fair."

"Tell that to Mr. Megabooks over

there," Howie suggested. "Obviously my fling with the magic wand didn't make any difference at all."

Liza, Melody, and Howie looked across the street while Eddie continued to read. Dozens of kids sat on the library steps reading while colorful banners blew all around them. Now there were two knights in shining armor walking along the sidewalk. Ladies in long dresses and pointed hats welcomed kids into the library. Mr. Merle stood beside the door with a clipboard, signing students up for his reading program. Mrs. Queen and the man in the velvet jogging suit stood next to him.

"Doesn't Mr. Merle know that you can get too much of a good thing?" Liza asked. "Reading *is* good, but not *all* the time."

"Well, I'm going to tell him," Melody said. She looked both ways, then stomped across the street and up the library steps.

Liza gulped. "I know Melody likes soccer as much as Eddie, but we've got to stop her before Mr. Merle turns her into fish stew."

"You're right," Howie said. He grabbed Eddie by the arm and they followed Melody across the street. Eddie never took his eyes off his book.

Melody was right in front of Mr. Merle when Liza and Howie stumbled up the first step. Eddie sat down and continued reading. Melody opened her mouth, ready to speak. But before she had a chance, a huge white van marked BCTV stopped in front of the library along with two big black cars. People swarmed out of the cars and cameras popped up all around the library steps.

A lady in a black suit marched up to Mr. Merle and shook his hand. "Congratulations on your reading program, it has been a great success. I'm with the State Library Department and would like you to work with us."

Mr. Merle smiled and touched his star necklace. "That would be delightful. I won't stop until kids all over the whole state have joined my Kingdom of Reading."

"Oh, no!" Howie said, slapping his hand against his face. "We're doomed."

Mr. Merle and the lady got in one of the black cars with Mrs. Queen and her friend while all the cameramen got back in the television van. They drove away and left everything quiet.

Liza sighed and watched the black car drive down the street. Then she whispered softly to herself, "It was nice for one brief shining moment to have a place called Camelot."

SLAM! Liza jumped as Eddie shut his book. He hopped up and bopped her on the head. "What did you say, noodle-nose?" Eddie asked.

Melody laughed. "Maybe the magic wand worked after all."

Debbie Dadey and Marcia Thornton Jones have fun writing stories together. When they both worked at an elementary school in Lexington, Kentucky, Debbie was the school librarian and Marcia was a teacher. During their lunch break in the school cafeteria, they came up with the idea of the Bailey School kids.

Recently Debbie and her family moved to Aurora, Illinois. Marcia and her husband still live in Kentucky where she continues to teach. How do these authors still write together? They talk on the phone and use computers and fax machines!